HOCKEY RULES!

The Official, Illustrated Kids' Guide to NHL® Rules and Regulations

by Dan Diamond

Grosset & Dunlap • New York

P9-CRQ-205

Published by Grosset & Dunlap, a division of Penguin Putnam Books for Young Readers. GROSSET & DUNLAP is a trademark of Penguin Putnam Inc.

Library of Congress Catalog Card Number: 00-108267

ISBN: 1-58184-101-9   10 9 8 7 6 5 4 3 2 1

Printed in the United States

Writers: Dan Diamond and Eric Zweig
Illustrator: Albert Molnar
Designer: fiwired.com

Photo Credits:
page 5, Hockey Hall of Fame; *page 6*, Hockey Hall of Fame; *page 7*, B. Bennett/Bruce Bennett Studios; *page 11*, M. Digiacomo/Bruce Bennett Studios; *page 16*, Imperial Oil–Turofsky/Hockey Hall of Fame; *page 17*, Hockey Hall of Fame; *page 19*, Hockey Hall of Fame; *page 22*, Hockey Hall of Fame; *page 25*, Hockey Hall of Fame; *page 43*, Brian Bahr/Allsport; *page 46*, J. McIsaac/Bruce Bennett Studios; *page 49*, Hockey Hall of Fame; *page 60*, Imperial Oil–Turofsky/Hockey Hall of Fame; *page 62*, Rick Stewart/Allsport

Contents

1 How Hockey Came to Be

People have played games on ice for hundreds of years. The first skates were made from bones or antlers that were tied with laces to the skaters' shoes or boots. Eventually, metal blades were attached to the skaters' footwear with straps and buckles. Sometimes, the blades were screwed right to the bottom of the boot. Pieter Brueghel, a famous

painter who lived in Holland more than four hundred years ago, created a picture called *Hunters in the Snow*. In the lower left-hand corner you can see a group of figures in the distance. They are wearing skates and, more importantly, carrying sticks with a crook at the end. People believe these sticks were used to whack a ball or disc along the ice.

James Creighton wrote the "Montreal Rules" for hockey, which laid the foundation for the modern game played today.

While Brueghel's picture may be one of the first paintings of a hockey game, it would take another 200 years for the sport to evolve into the organized game we play today.

Organized hockey's roots can be traced to Eastern Canada. Soldiers in Halifax, Nova Scotia, and Kingston, Ontario, devised on-ice versions of the games they had played at home in England, Scotland, and Ireland. They called these games ice rugby, ice polo, ice hurley, or ice hockey. One of the early Nova Scotia players was James Creighton. When he moved to Montreal in the early 1870s, he took his passion for the new ice games with him. His Montreal friends, who already knew how to skate, were fascinated with the games and asked Creighton to write down a set of rules.

Borrowing heavily from the game of rugby, Creighton wrote what came to be known as the "Montreal Rules." Forward passing was not permitted, and the ball had to be passed back or sideways. (Later, the top and bottom would be cut off the ball to keep it from bouncing over the low boards used to frame the rink. This cut-down ball soon came to be known as the "puck," after an Irish word—sometime spelled "puc"—meaning "smack" or "hit.") There were nine players on each team, one referee, and two goal judges. The goal judges had to be especially brave—they stood right on the ice behind and between the goal posts. There wasn't a net or a crossbar, just two posts sticking up from the ice.

Montreal Rules hockey was an instant hit. Games were played every day at the city's new Victoria Rink. In fact, the matches were so popular the *Montreal Gazette* newspaper began to run articles on them in 1875. A new sport was born. Today—125 years later—the games you play on your local rink and the games played in packed NHL arenas are the direct result of the games played by James Creighton and his friends.

Almost everyone has dreamed of getting into a time machine, spinning the dials, and ending up in another time and place. If you went back to Montreal in 1875 to see James Creighton and his friends playing their new game, the action would certainly be much slower than what you see today. The rutted ice and flat, wobbly skate blades slowed the play, and players never got a chance to rest (there were no substitutions). Today's players go all-out for 45 seconds and then head to the bench. The whole game is played at top speed. Smooth ice, high-tech skates, and bigger, stronger players make for a lightning-fast game.

Have any elements from the 1875 game survived? The basic objective has never changed. Teams are still trying to score more goals than

Even "Mr. Hockey," the great Gordie Howe, needed help from teammates to score his 802 career goals.

6

their opponents. Hockey is still based on flow: The action never stops. If the puck is frozen, the whistle blows and the play starts again. It's right in the *National Hockey League Official Rules:* "Rule 79(a) The puck must be kept in motion at all times." Most importantly, however, hockey in 1875 and in 2000 stresses team play—no player can do it by himself. Even the greatest superstars, whether it was Gordie Howe or Wayne Gretzky, needed someone to pass them the puck or someone to pass the puck to. Hockey was, and still is, a team game.

When it's played well, hockey requires its players to be quick, strong, smart, and brave. To be part of a team. To think and create on the ice. To give a pass or take a check for the good of the team. Every time you lace up your skates, you can be part of some hockey magic: By working with each other, you and your teammates can be better together than you might be as individual players. Often in hockey, the best *team* beats the best *individual players*. James Creighton surely learned this in 1875, and it remains true today.

Hockey can be a beautiful game, but, as in all sports, people can get hurt. Especially when they break the rules. When you have hard ice, solid boards, and players with long sticks in their hands skating at high speeds, you have to be careful. So how do you experience the beautiful part of hockey and reduce your risk of getting hurt?

Wayne Gretzky was the ultimate team player. His assists (1,963) were more than double his goals (894).

1

1. Wear proper equipment and wear your equipment properly. In particular, wear a helmet with the chin strap done up, have a mask that fits, and use a mouth guard.

2. Know what's going on. Be in the game by knowing where the puck is and where your opponents are at all times. It's better to be part of the play than to be drifting around the ice without a clue.

3. Be physically fit and learn the fundamentals of the game. If you're in shape and are a good skater, you won't get tired and caught out of position—a situation where players often get hurt. You want to be hockey smart, too. This means anticipating where the puck is most likely to go and working with your teammates to make the most of your opportunities. Your coach can help as well. He or she can tell you how the game works so you can improve as a player and as a member of your team.

4. Respect everyone on the ice, including yourself. You all have three things in common: You are there because you like to play hockey, you are trying to win, and you are hoping to play in many

I DID NOT KNOW THAT.

more hockey games. With this much in common, you have the basis for respect; you might even become friends.

5. Follow the rules. Even if you think the referee isn't looking, even if you think you can get away with it, deliberately violating the rules isn't right—it goes against the true spirit of the game. Hockey is about having a good time and playing your best while following the rules. Hockey isn't about cheating.

So how do you follow the rules? First, you learn what the rules are and why they were created. If you do this, you'll have learned a lot about hockey and its history. You'll be a better player and you'll be a smarter fan, whether you are watching a game in the arena or at home on TV. To help you, we've prepared this book, *Hockey Rules!*

Enjoy the book and, more importantly, enjoy every hockey experience in your life.

2   Principles of Play

Hockey is simple: You and your teammates are trying to put the puck in the opposing team's net while preventing your opponents from scoring on you. Unless there are penalties, each team has six players on the ice at one time (see Rule 13a): a goaltender, two defensemen, and a forward line made up of a left winger, a center, and a right winger. The ice is divided into three zones (see Rule 5). The area from your net out to your blue line is the *defensive zone*. The *neutral zone* extends from blue line to blue line. Lastly, the area from the opposing blue line to the opposing net is the *attacking zone*.

With the exception of the goaltender, whose job is to prevent the opposing team from scoring, every player has both offensive and defensive responsibilities in all three zones.

Defensemen have to be able to skate strongly both forward and backward. Their job is to prevent opposing puck carriers from skating in on their net in the defensive zone. They challenge the opposing forwards when they attack, looking to block or deflect shots on goal. When the defensemen gain possession of the puck, they often carry it out of their own end through the neutral zone before passing it to one of their forwards. If the opportunity presents itself, they might lead the attack by going right to the net. Sometimes, if the forwards have carried the puck in, a defenseman might follow in late to become the "trailer," looking for a pass, a rebound, or a loose puck.

Forwards do the bulk of the scoring on any hockey team. They carry the puck through the neutral zone and rush into the opponent's end, looking for a scoring chance through a smart pass or a shot on goal. They often have to work in the corners against an opponent to dig out the puck for their linemates. The center is also responsible for taking face-offs in all three zones.

Forwards have important defensive responsibilities, too. When the opposing team gets possession of the puck and brings it up ice, forwards support their defensemen. The forwards check their opponents and look to break up the rush by intercepting a pass. If the puck gets loose in the defensive zone, it's the job of the forwards to get in position to receive a pass from the defense to begin a rush the other way.

Guiding all of this swirling motion is the coaching staff. Sometimes it's one person, sometimes there are two or three people behind the bench. The coaching staff is responsible for deciding who is on the ice and for dictating team strategy on things like face-offs. Games are often won or lost by the decisions coaches make.

Bobby Orr was a rare player—a gifted defenseman with the ability to move the puck and score.

3   Setting the Stage

The Rink

The National Hockey League was established in 1917, but no rink dimensions were included as part of the *National Hockey League Official Rules* until 1929–30. In 1929, the rinks were officially made 200 feet long and 85 feet wide. These dimensions remain in use to this day (see Rule 2a). Three NHL arenas had dimensions that differed: Boston Garden was 191 feet by 88 feet; Chicago Stadium was 188 feet by 85 feet; and Buffalo's War Memorial Auditorium was 193 feet by 84 feet. All three of these grand old rinks were replaced by new arenas in the 1990s. Their replacements—the Fleet Center in Boston, the United Center in Chicago, and the HSBC Arena in Buffalo—are regulation size.

International hockey has its own rules. One of the major differences between international and North American hockey is the size of the rink. International hockey is played on an ice surface that is 200 feet long by 100 feet wide. The wider international ice surface gives players more room to skate and pass, and in part explains why international hockey has less bodychecking than the North American game.

The markings on a hockey rink have undergone great changes over the years. When the NHL first began in 1917, the only face-off dot was at center ice. Blue lines, face-off circles, goal creases, and the center ice red line were all added at different times between 1918 and 1943. The ice surface was painted white in 1949. Before that time, the ice had no color of its own and usually looked dark gray, owing to the color of the arena floor beneath the ice surface. During games, the gray surface would be covered with white patches of snow scraped from the ice by

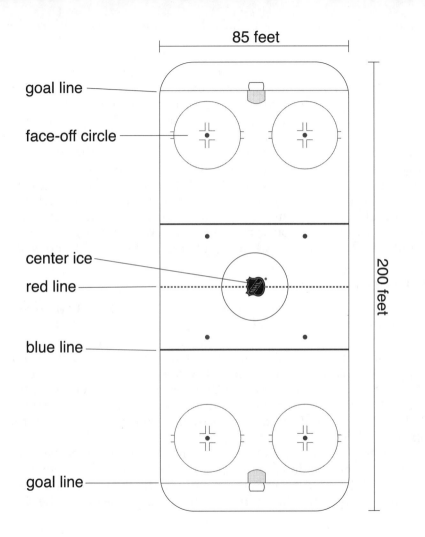

85 feet

200 feet

goal line

face-off circle

center ice

red line

blue line

goal line

the players' skates, making it difficult to follow the puck. When the United States first began to televise hockey games in the late 1940s, and Canada followed suit in the early 1950s, the white ice surface made the game much brighter and the puck easier to follow.

The most recent change to the markings on the ice occurred in 1998–99, when the goal crease was modified from a full semicircle to one that had its ends chopped off (see Rule 4). The goal crease is important because it defines a safe area for the goaltender where opposing players can't interfere with his efforts to stop the puck. If an attacking player is in the crease when a goal is scored, the referee can disallow the goal if he feels that the player interfered with the goalie.

To aid the referee and the video goal judge in making decisions about goals, the crease area is painted light blue, while the area inside the net is white. The puck must be fully over the red goal line to count, so if you don't see white ice all around the puck, it's no goal.

Players on the Ice

The NHL has always played six-man hockey (see Rule 13a), except during the Stanley Cup Playoffs between 1918 and 1922. In those years, the Stanley Cup was awarded to the winner of a series between the champions of the NHL and the champions of the Pacific Coast Hockey Association (PCHA). The PCHA had different rules than those of the NHL. Most importantly, it played seven-man hockey. One extra skater, known as the rover, lined up midway between the forwards and the defense, and roved all over the ice, contributing to both the offense and defense.

During the Stanley Cup series, games would alternate between the rules of the two different leagues, so when PCHA rules were used, the NHL club would have to add the rover. The PCHA stopped using the rover prior to the start of the 1922–23 season. The last professional game played under seven-man rules took place on March 25, 1922, when the Toronto St. Pats defeated the Vancouver Millionaires by a 6–0 score.

Uniforms

Hockey was one of the first team sports to have its players wear numbers. The PCHA used them first in 1911, and when the NHL was formed in 1917, all players were required to wear numbers on the back of their jerseys. Numbers were added to the sides of players' skates and to the sleeves of their jerseys in the 1950s, making it easier to identify players in newspaper photos and on television. (See Rule 13b.)

Today's rules require players' names to be on the back of their sweaters, both at home and on the road (see Rule 13b). Teams were first allowed to add players' names to their home uniforms in 1970, and to road uniforms in 1978. The 1975 Stanley Cup Finals between the Buffalo Sabres and the Philadelphia Flyers anticipated this change—both teams wore names on their jerseys for the series.

Team Captains

Team captains have been part of hockey since the game's earliest days, when they often served as a playing coach. NHL rules have always prohibited this double duty for fear that if a captain/coach was ejected from the game, the penalized team would be leaderless (see Rule 14d). In 1946, the NHL introduced a rule that required the captain to wear a "C" on the front of his uniform. Alternate captains were required to wear an "A" (see Rule 14a). In European hockey, the captain often wears an armband like in soccer. Russian teams use a "K" to indicate their captain rather than a "C."

Prior to 1948, six goaltenders had served as team captains, but a rule passed that year prohibited goaltenders from wearing the "C" or the "A" (see Rule 14d). It was felt that having a goaltender leave his crease to discuss things with the referee would delay the game and was almost like creating an unofficial time-out. Bill Durnan of the Canadiens was the last goaltender to serve as his team's captain. He shared the role with teammate Elmer Lach during the 1947–48 season.

Players on a Team

In the NHL today, each team may dress 18 skaters and two goaltenders for every game. However, the number of players in uniform for each game has changed many times over the years. In the 1952–53 season, teams were permitted to dress 16 skaters at home but only 15 on the road. In 1954–55, the number of players in uniform was set at 18 players plus a goaltender for the first two months of the season but was then cut back to 16 players plus a goaltender for the rest of the schedule, starting on December 1, 1954.

Prior to the 1950s, teams carried only one goaltender. If he was injured, it was a position player—usually a defenseman—who took over in net. Lester Patrick, a 44-year-old retired star player who was coach of the New York Rangers, took over for injured goaltender Lorne Chabot late in the first period of a game in the 1928 Stanley Cup Finals.

Patrick's team won the game 2–1 and would go on to win the Stanley Cup.

Throughout the 1950s, each NHL team had to have a substitute goalie on hand for home games in case either team's regular goaltender was injured. If an injury occurred, the "house goalie" would come out of the stands, put on his equipment and the jersey of the team he'd be playing for, get warmed up, and play. It could take at least 20 minutes for the goalie to get ready. The house goalies were usually junior, senior, or minor pro goaltenders. Occasionally, team trainers doubled as practice goalies for the home team. Television, however, ended the era of the house goalie. The long delay was unacceptable, so in 1965–66 a new rule required every team to dress two goaltenders for every game (see Rule 15d). Many clubs were already using a two-goalie system when the rule was enacted—though until the new rule came into effect, they could only dress one for each game.

The last position player to spend time in net was Jerry Toppazzini of the Boston Bruins, who played the last few seconds of a 5–2 loss to Chicago on October 16, 1960.

Changing Players

In the early days of hockey, few substitutions were made. Lester Patrick made hockey history in the 1925 Stanley Cup Finals when he used frequent line changes to keep his players fresh, enabling the Victoria Cougars of the Western Canada Hockey League to defeat the speedy Montreal Canadiens. This was the last time that a non-NHL team won the Stanley Cup. Since 1927, only NHL teams have played for the trophy.

One of the players who played in that 1925 series was Odie Cleghorn. The following season, he coached Pittsburgh's first entry in the NHL, a team named the Pirates. Cleghorn's Pirates perfected changing "on the fly," enabling the coach to use all of the players on his bench. Because the Pirates were a new club with few real stars, it was important to keep everybody fresh and at their peak during each game.

Changing on the fly wasn't really legal until the *National Hockey League Official Rules* was amended in 1927, but Cleghorn's approach was seen as the wave of the future. Eventually, the rule would be written so that a substitute could come on if the player he was replacing was within five feet of the players' bench. Today, it is the linesman's job to make sure that this rule is followed. If a player jumps on the ice too soon, play is whistled dead and a penalty is called for having too many men on the ice (see Rule 17).

Equipment

Sticks

The first rule on stick length was passed in 1927 and restricted sticks to no more than 53 inches in length. Ernie "Moose" Johnson, who played defense and forward in the Pacific Coast Hockey Association long before the NHL enacted its first stick rule, used a stick 75 inches long and was said to have a reach of 99 inches! Today, the maximum allowable length of a stick is 63 inches, and the stick blade can be no more than 12½ inches from heel to toe (see Rule 19b).

Curved stick blades first found their way into use in the late 1950s. Andy Bathgate of the New York Rangers, and Bobby Hull and Stan Mikita of the Chicago Blackhawks are credited with being the first to use them. They would hold their stick blades over steam from a boiling kettle, soak them in hot water, and then wedge them under the bottom of a door and pull up to give them the curve they wanted. They found that a curved stick gave them a faster shot that dipped in flight, making the puck harder for the goalie to stop.

More and more players started to use the "banana blades," which were soon being supplied by the stick manufacturers with the curve already in place. Almost every top scorer used a curve by the middle of the 1960s, and

Bobby Hull had one of the hardest shots in the NHL, thanks, in part, to his curved blade.

almost every goaltender now wore a mask—shots from the banana blades were unpredictable because of the way they would dip and dart. The maximum allowable curve was set at one inch in 1967–68 and reduced to half an inch in 1970–71, where it has remained to this day (see Rule 19b).

Referees have a special tool that measures a stick blade to see if it has an illegal curve. A player caught using an illegal stick is given a minor penalty. A coach can request that an opposing player's stick be measured. If the referee finds that the stick being measured is legal, the team that asked for the measurement is penalized for delay of game (see Rule 19d). As a result, coaches are very careful to only ask for a stick measurement at important moments in a game.

The most important stick measurement in modern hockey history took place in Game 2 of the 1993 Stanley Cup Finals between the Los Angeles Kings and the Montreal Canadiens. The Kings had won Game 1 and were leading the second game by a score of 2–1 late in the third period. Canadiens coach Jacques Demers did not want to go down two games to none, so he asked for a stick measurement on Kings defenseman Marty McSorley. The stick was found to be illegal, so a penalty was called. The Canadiens scored on the powerplay and then won the game in overtime, with Eric Desjardins getting both the tying and winning goals. Montreal went on to win the Stanley Cup in five games. Without the illegal stick penalty call against the Kings, Montreal might never have gotten on track and Los Angeles could have won its first Stanley Cup title.

Skates

Today's plastic moldings that hold the blade to the boot of the skate were introduced in the 1970s. Before that, players wore what were called tube skates. Tube skates were invented in Norway and brought to Canada in the early 1900s. They featured a sharp steel blade welded to a steel tube. In turn, the steel tube was riveted to the heel and toe of the skate boot. With the blade beneath the tube, skaters had better balance and could turn more quickly than ever before. The Winnipeg Victorias hockey club won the Stanley Cup in 1901 wearing tube skates, which gave them an advantage over their opponents who still wore old-fashioned, one-piece blades attached directly to the boot. Tube skates had a dangerous sharp point at the back of blade, so the NHL passed a rule in 1964 that required all players to wear an approved plastic heel guard. Today's skates no longer have this sharp point, but all skates still must have an approved safety blade (see Rule 20a).

Goaltending Equipment

With the exception of skates and sticks, all equipment worn by the goaltender must be constructed for the purpose of protecting the head or body. The goaltender must not wear any piece of equipment that would give him an unfair advantage in stopping pucks.

Goaltenders, however, have always been innovators. Emile Francis was Chicago's goaltender in 1947–48, when he appeared in goal using a first baseman's trapper on his catching hand. The opposing manager protested the use of this "unfair" equipment, but NHL president Clarence Campbell approved the new innovation.

George "Whitey" Merritt of the Winnipeg Victorias was the first goaltender to wear leg guards, using cricket pads in the Stanley Cup matches in February 1896. Modern goalie pads trace their roots to the early 1920s when Emil "Pop" Kenesky, a harness maker from Hamilton, Ontario, set out to improve the design by adding extra padding. Kenesky's pads became the standard by which all others

Carl Brewer, with the palms cut out of his gloves, slips the puck past goaltender Glenn Hall. Eventually, cut-out gloves were banned from the NHL.

were measured. Although modern goalie pads are made of lightweight materials, they still look similar to the Kenesky design. The maximum width of a goalie's pads is 12 inches per pad (see Rule 21b).

Throughout the late 1990s, scoring declined in the NHL. There were several reasons, but one was definitely that goalie equipment had become bigger and lighter, enabling the goalie to cover more of the net. Recent rule changes restrict the size of the goalie's shoulder pads, jersey, and catching glove (see Rule 21c-g).

Protective Equipment

Elbow pads were introduced in the 1940s and were first worn outside the jersey. These outside pads gradually became bigger and harder, and were believed to be causing injuries, not preventing them. Consequently, a rule was created in 1945 stating that, with the exception of helmets and gloves, all protective equipment must be worn under the uniform. Whether worn inside or outside of the jersey, hard elbow pads remained controversial in the NHL until a rule was passed in 1958, which prohibited any equipment that was likely to cause injury.

Helmets were also controversial, only because most players didn't wear them and didn't want to wear them in the early days of hockey. This started to change in 1979, when the NHL introduced a rule requiring all new players to wear helmets. Today, all NHL players wear helmets. In 1996–97, when Craig MacTavish retired from the St. Louis Blues, he was the last bare-headed player in the NHL.

Another rule prohibits the use of gloves with the palm cut out. Toronto Maple Leafs defenseman Carl Brewer used gloves without palms in 1960–61. The gloves gave him an advantage because he could grab onto an opponent's sweater without seeming to do so. Almost every opposing general manager protested Brewer's trick, so the NHL outlawed these cut-out gloves.

The Puck

The puck is made of rubber. It is one inch thick and three inches in diameter, weighing between five and one-half ounces and six ounces. Pucks used in games are frozen to reduce their bounce (see Rule 24). Today, the referee gets new pucks at the penalty bench, but before 1964–65, it was the home team's trainer that supplied the referee with frozen pucks as required. If the home team was leading a close game with just a few minutes left, the trainer would slip in an unfrozen puck. The unfrozen puck was more difficult to control, making it tougher for the visitors to score.

One of the milestone pucks at the Hockey Hall of Fame comes from a game on November 10, 1979, between the Minnesota North Stars and the Los Angeles Kings. This special puck was used for the whole game. It never went into the crowd. Usually more than a dozen pucks are used in a single game.

A high-tech puck was introduced in 1995–96 for use during games broadcast on TV by Fox Sports. This special puck looked normal to the players and fans in the arena but was surrounded by a blue glow or a red streak when viewed on television. Some people liked the effect and some hated it, but it certainly received lots of publicity around the world. When ABC and ESPN took over American hockey broadcasts in 1999, they did not use the so-called "glowing puck."

Penalties

Penalties have been part of hockey since its earliest days. Tripping, kicking, charging, high-sticking, shoving, and collaring were prohibited in a set of rules published in Montreal in 1886. At that time, the referee was instructed to issue a player with two warnings. If the player committed a third offense, the referee kicked him out of the game.

There have been 65 penalty-free games in the NHL, the most recent taking place in a match between Colorado and Detroit on April 9, 2000. In 1944, a unique game occurred between the Chicago Blackhawks and the Toronto Maple Leafs. No goals were scored and no penalties were called. The game lasted less than two hours.

Minor Penalties

The first recorded mention of minor penalties is found in a 1904 newspaper report. Back then, referees were allowed to call penalties of two, three, or five minutes at their discretion. Beginning in 1914, all penalties were five minutes long, but the penalized team was allowed to replace the player in the penalty box so they didn't have to play one man short. Penalties were reduced to three minutes in 1916–17. When the NHL began play in 1917–18, three-minute minors were called, but the penalized team played a man short for the whole three minutes. The two-minute minor that we use today was first whistled in 1921–22.

The mighty 1955–56 Montreal Canadiens had such a strong powerplay, the NHL changed the existing rule to allow penalized players back on the ice if a goal was scored.

Since the 1956–57 season, a rule has allowed the penalized player to return to the ice if his team is scored upon (see Rule 26c). The thinking was that giving up a goal was a big enough penalty for a minor offense. This rule is still known as the "Montreal Canadiens rule" because the 1955–56 Habs had such a strong powerplay that it sometimes scored more than one goal during a two-minute advantage. On November 5, 1955, center Jean Beliveau of the Canadiens scored three powerplay goals in 44 seconds against Boston. The rule change diminished Montreal's advantage.

Until 1985, if both teams were penalized at the same time, the players would go to the penalty box and the two teams would both play a man short. Beginning with the 1985–86 season, a rule was passed that allowed teams to substitute for these players, keeping the play at five skaters (not including the goalie) against five. This rule change had a special name, too. It was known as the "Edmonton Oilers rule." The Oilers were so powerful on offense that playing four skaters against four gave them a big advantage. With the extra space, Oilers players like Wayne Gretzky, Jari Kurri, Mark Messier, Glenn Anderson, and Paul Coffey scored many powerplay goals.

The "Edmonton Oilers rule" was changed back to the old system in 1992–93 (see Rule 26d). By this time, Wayne Gretzky had left Edmonton, and the NHL wanted to give fans more to cheer about by increasing the number of goals scored.

Major Penalties

Major penalties are five minutes in length. Unlike a minor penalty, a player in the penalty box for a major does not come back on the ice if the other team scores. Almost every category of minor penalty—tripping, charging, high-sticking—can be called as a major at the discretion of the referee. A five-minute major is the minimum penalty that can be called for fighting.

If a high-sticking incident results in an injury to the head or the face of an opposing player, the player receiving a major penalty also receives a fine of $100 (see Rule 27a).

Any player who receives three major penalties in one game is suspended for the rest of the game and must pay a fine of $200 (see Rule 27b).

Any player who receives a major penalty for butt-ending, checking from behind, clipping, cross-checking, hooking, slashing, or spearing is suspended for the rest of the game and must pay a fine of $200 (see Rule 27b).

Misconduct Penalties

Misconducts are given by the referee to a player on the ice, or to a player or coach on the bench, for verbally or physically abusing the officials. Many misconducts are given to players who continue to argue or scuffle when the referee tells them to stop. Misconduct penalties are 10 minutes long, and teams are allowed to use a substitute for the penalized player (see Rule 28).

Match Penalties

A match penalty results in a player being removed from the game. It is called when a play on the ice is particularly violent, or if an offense has occurred repeatedly. If a match penalty is called for attempting to injure an opponent, for deliberately injuring an opponent, or for kicking, the team whose player has been kicked out has to play a man short for five minutes (see Rule 29).

Ten minutes is added to the penalty record of any player receiving a match penalty. Every time a match penalty is called, the referee who calls the penalty submits a report to the Commissioner of the NHL, explaining what happened. Sometimes, additional suspensions or fines result from the incident.

Penalty Shots

A penalty shot can be awarded for a variety of reasons, but the most common is when a player who has a breakaway or a clear scoring chance is tripped from behind. The player who was pulled down gets to take the penalty shot, and all the other players—except the goalie—skate to their respective benches. The referee puts the puck at center ice. Then, the player taking the penalty shot picks up the puck and skates in on the opposing goaltender. He can shoot whenever he wants, as long as he doesn't cross the goal line. The player has to keep skating forward, and he can't score on a rebound. If the puck hits the goal post, or bounces off the goaltender, and then goes in, the goal counts.

The NHL first awarded penalty shots in 1934–35. Over the years, the way shots were taken and the reasons they were awarded changed many times. Until 1938–39, penalty shots were taken from a 10-foot circle painted on the ice 38 feet from the goal. The shooter couldn't touch the puck once it left the 10-foot circle, so it was a true penalty shot similar to a penalty kick in soccer. After the change in 1938–39, penalty shots were taken in a way that was similar to today's system. The player taking the shot could carry the puck in and do his best to put it by the goaltender from any point.

There were two kinds of penalty shots from 1941–42 to 1944–45: minor and major. Minor penalty shots were awarded when goaltenders committed an infraction. They were taken from a line painted on the ice 28 feet in front of the goal. Major penalty shots were awarded when skaters committed an infraction. They were taken in a way that was similar to today's penalty shot.

Beginning in 1945–46, all penalty shots were taken from the far blue line with the player being allowed to skate right in on the goalie. The starting point changed to center ice in 1962–63 (see Rule 30a).

In the modern NHL, approximately 20 penalty shots are taken each season. The goalie stops the shot approximately 60 percent of the time (see "Penalty Shot Table" on next page).

Penalty Shot Table

Season	Shots	Goals	Scoring %	Season	Shots	Goals	Scoring %
1934-35	29	4	13.8	1967-68	8	2	25.0
1935-36	5	4	80.0	1968-69	4	1	25.0
1936-37	1	1	100.0	1969-70	3	0	0.0
1937-38	8	1	12.5	1970-71	5	2	40.0
1938-39	3	1	33.3	1971-72	9	3	33.3
1939-40	2	2	100.0	1972-73	8	2	25.0
1940-41	2	1	50.0	1973-74	13	5	38.5
1941-42	7	7	100.0	1974-75	14	6	42.9
1942-43	3	2	66.6	1975-76	11	1	9.1
1943-44	3	1	33.3	1976-77	13	5	38.5
1944-45	4	3	75.0	1977-78	14	2	14.3
1945-46	3	2	66.6	1978-79	10	2	20.0
1946-47	0	0	0.0	1979-80	14	5	35.7
1947-48	1	0	0.0	1980-81	12	3	25.0
1948-49	2	1	50.0	1981-82	9	5	55.6
1949-50	2	2	100.0	1982-83	15	6	40.0
1950-51	1	0	0.0	1983-84	18	10	55.6
1951-52	1	1	100.0	1984-85	19	9	47.4
1952-53	2	2	100.0	1985-86	15	6	40.0
1953-54	0	0	0.0	1986-87	25	13	52.0
1954-55	1	0	0.0	1987-88	21	9	42.9
1955-56	0	0	0.0	1988-89	26	7	27.0
1956-57	1	1	100.0	1989-90	16	6	37.5
1957-58	0	0	0.0	1990-91	20	9	45.0
1958-59	0	0	0.0	1991-92	29	12	41.4
1959-60	1	0	0.0	1992-93	30	14	46.7
1960-61	0	0	0.0	1993-94	27	11	40.7
1961-62	10	4	40.0	1994-95	17	3	17.6
1962-63	4	1	25.0	1995-96	27	5	18.5
1963-64	9	4	44.4	1996-97	24	10	41.6
1964-65	3	2	66.6	1997-98	34	16	47.1
1965-66	0	0	0.0	1998-99	27	11	40.7
1966-67	7	4	57.1	1999-2000	40	16	40.0

❸ Goaltender's Penalties

Goaltenders are subject to the same rules as other players. A goaltender can't trip, high-stick, or spear an opponent. The difference, however, is that a goaltender does not serve any penalties called on him by the referee. He stays on while his penalty is served by another member of his team—someone who was on the ice when the penalty was called.

Goaltenders have several unique penalties. A minor penalty for delay of game (see Rule 51a) is automatically called if a goaltender shoots the puck over the glass. A goaltender also earns a minor penalty if he skates over the center red line (see Rule 31i).

Calling Penalties

Hockey officials use a system of hand signals to indicate to the fans, players, coaches, and penalty timekeeper which infraction has been called. These signals were devised by Bill Chadwick, an NHL referee in the 1940s. They proved popular with fans who often didn't know which penalty had been called. By the end of the decade, a system of hand signals based on Chadwick's was being used throughout the NHL.

When the referee sees that a penalty has been committed, he waits until the team that got the penalty touches the puck before he blows his whistle. Once the whistle has been blown, the referee signals the appropriate penalty and skates over to the penalty timekeeper's bench to tell him the number of the player who received the penalty, the number of penalty minutes, and the penalty called. He might say, "Number 20, blue. Two for tripping." A few moments later, the public address announcer will tell the crowd, "Detroit penalty, number 20, Bill Player, two minutes for tripping. Time of the penalty 6 minutes, 43 seconds. Player, two minutes for tripping." Games played in the Molson Centre in Montreal announce penalties and goals in Canada's two official languages: French, followed by English. Canada's two official languages are also used at the Corel Centre in Ottawa; but there, it is English followed by French.

The referee can call many different kinds of penalties. Usually he must decide whether the infraction warrants a two-minute minor penalty, a four-minute double minor, or a five-minute major. Every infraction has its own hand signal.

Boarding (see Rule 44) is called when a player checks an opponent in a manner that causes the opponent to be thrown violently into the boards.

Charging (see Rule 47) is called when a player "runs at" an opponent (skates hard over a distance toward him) and violently checks him. This can happen anywhere on the ice.

Cross-checking (see Rule 50) is called when a player has both of his hands on the stick and his arms extended while checking an opponent.

Elbowing (see Rule 53) is called when a player extends his elbow to check or impede an opponent in what the referee judges to be a careless or dangerous manner.

High-sticking (see Rule 61) is called when a player makes contact with an opponent with a stick carried above the height of the opponent's shoulders.

3

Holding (see Rule 62) is called when a player uses his hands, arms, or legs to hold an opponent.

Hooking (see Rule 64) is called when a player uses his stick to slow down or restrain an opponent.

Interference (see Rule 67 and 88a) is called when a player interferes with, checks, or impedes the progress of an opponent who does not have possession of the puck.

Kneeing (see Rule 71) is called when a player uses his raised knee to check or impede an opponent.

Roughing (see Rule 84) is called when a player is involved in a minor altercation that stops short of earning a major penalty for fighting. A roughing minor is the minimum penalty that can be called when a player strikes an opponent.

Slashing (see Rule 85) is called when a player swings his stick at an opponent. The penalty is called even if contact is not made.

Spearing (see Rule 86) is called when a player uses the point of his stick blade to stab at an opponent. The minimum penalty for spearing is a double minor.

Tripping (see Rule 91) is called when a player uses his stick or a portion of his body to cause his opponent to trip and fall. If, in the opinion of the referee, a player is clearly attempting to gain possession of the puck and trips an opponent as he gains possession, no penalty will be called.

Unsportsmanlike conduct (see Rule 41) is called when a player challenges or disputes an official's ruling, or when a player uses abusive language or gestures.

Officials

In addition to the two teams playing on the ice, there's a third team at every NHL game: the officials. Each game is worked by four on-ice officials (two referees and two linesmen) and seven off-ice officials (two goal judges, one game timekeeper, one penalty timekeeper, one official scorer, one statistician, and one video goal judge). (See Rule 34.) The home team provides the off-ice officials for regular-season games. The NHL assigns out-of-town off-ice officials during the playoffs. Until 1945–46, the home team also provided the linesmen.

The use of two referees is a recent innovation in the NHL—used for many regular season games and all playoff games in both the 1998–99 and 1999–2000 seasons. Beginning in 2000–2001, every game will use two referees.

The referees supervise the game. They have control of the other officials, and of the players and coaches on both teams. A referee's decision is final.

The referee orders the teams onto the ice to begin the game or the period. He checks that all players are wearing proper equipment and uniforms. He ensures that the off-ice officials are in place, and that the time clock and the goal lights are working properly. The referee drops the puck for the face-off at the beginning of each period and after a goal has been scored.

The referee calls any penalties that he thinks are required. He makes the final decision when goals are disputed, consulting with the other referee, linesmen, goal judge, and video goal judge as required. It is the referee who tells the official scorer the number of the player who scores. The official scorer has the job of awarding assists when a goal is scored.

At the end of a game, it is the referee who checks the final game report and team rosters, and signs them before they are submitted to the NHL office.

The linesmen have the difficult job of deciding if plays are offside. The basic offside rule (see Rule 74) states that when a team carries the puck into the attacking zone, the puck must cross the blue line before all the skaters from the attacking team. When this happens, the play is "onside" and is allowed to continue. When it doesn't, the play is "offside," and it is the linesman's job to blow the whistle and stop play. The linesman also stops play when icing has occurred. Icing is called when a player on one team shoots the puck from his team's side of center ice all the way down the ice and across the other team's goal line. In the NHL, when a member of the opposing team touches the puck, the linesman whistles and stops the play with an icing call. The puck is brought back down the ice for a face-off.

The linesmen drop the puck at all face-offs not handled by the referee.

Linesmen can also stop play for several reasons—if the net has been dislodged, if too many men are on the ice, or when a double minor penalty is called for butt-ending, head-butting, high-sticking, or spearing. The linesmen also have the difficult job of separating players involved in altercations after the whistle. The referees leave this job to the linesmen so they can watch what is going on and call penalties if any are required.

Playing Rules 4

To read the latest version of every NHL rule, you need to get the current edition of the *National Hockey League Official Rules*. Section Six covers the official playing rules. Many of the rules are presented here, along with an explanation of how they work and how they came to be.

<u>Rule 42.</u> Adjustment to Clothing or Equipment

(a) *Play shall not be stopped nor the game delayed for adjustments to clothing, equipment, skates, or sticks. For an infringement of the rule, a two-minute penalty shall be given.*

(b) *If adjustments are required, the player shall leave the ice and play shall continue with a substitute.*

(c) *No delay shall be permitted for the repair or adjustment of a goalkeeper's equipment. If adjustments are required, the goalkeeper shall leave the ice, and his place shall be taken by the substitute goalkeeper immediately.*

Rule 42 was introduced to help speed up the tempo of the game and to prevent players from taking an "unofficial" time-out when their team was in trouble. Back in 1927, the original rule allowed goalies to fix their equipment, but since 1974–75 goalies must make repairs on the bench, while play continues with the substitute goalie.

<u>Rule 43.</u> Attempt to Injure

(a) *A match penalty shall be called on any player who deliberately attempts to injure an opponent, and the circumstances shall be reported to the Commissioner for further action.*

(b) *A game misconduct shall be called on any player who deliberately attempts to injure an official, manager, coach, or trainer in any manner, and the circumstances shall be reported to the Commissioner for further action.*

Attempt to injure is one of the most serious infractions in the *National Hockey League Official Rules,* and is punishable by penalties and suspensions. When Marty McSorley hit Donald Brashear in the head with his stick on February 21, 2000, he was penalized under the attempt to injure rule. McSorley's subsequent suspension was the longest in NHL history for an on-ice incident.

<u>Rule 45.</u> Broken Stick

(a) *A player whose stick is broken may participate in the game provided he drops the broken stick. A two-minute penalty shall be imposed for an infraction of this rule.*

(b) *A goalkeeper may continue to play with a broken stick until a stoppage of play or until he has been legally given a new stick.*

(c) *A player who has lost or broken his stick may only receive a stick at his own players' bench or be handed one from a teammate on the ice.*

He cannot receive a new stick from a teammate in the penalty box. A two-minute penalty shall be imposed for an infraction of this rule.

<u>Note:</u> *A player who picks up a stick that has been thrown on the ice from the players' or penalty bench will not receive a penalty, but the player who threw the stick will.*

(d) *A goalkeeper whose stick is broken will receive a penalty if he goes to the bench to receive a new one. He must receive his replacement stick from a teammate.*

In the early days of hockey, sticks were much heavier than they are today and very difficult to break. Players could use them for years. Still, because of the risk of injury to others on the ice, at no time in hockey history has a player—other than a goaltender—been allowed to play with a broken stick. In fact, until the 1940s, players had to go to the bench immediately once their stick was broken and either be replaced by a teammate or grab a new stick. Midway through the 1946–47 season, the rule was changed to allow players to remain on the ice without a stick. Goalies had always been allowed to stay on the ice, but until the rules were changed in 1946–47, they were not allowed to use any part of their broken stick. Today, a goaltender can play with a broken stick until play stops. When the whistle blows, one of his teammates must bring him a new stick from the players' bench.

A STICK, A STICK, MY KINGDOM FOR A STICK!

Playing Rules

<u>Rule 48.</u> Checking from Behind

(a) *Any player who cross-checks, pushes, or charges from behind an opponent who is unable to defend himself shall be given a five-minute major penalty and a game misconduct.*

(b) *Any player who receives two game misconducts for checking from behind either during the regular season or in the playoffs will automatically be suspended for his team's next game. For each additional game misconduct the player is given, the suspension is increased by one game.*

A check from behind is considered to be a check delivered to a player who is not aware he is about to be hit and so cannot protect himself when contact is made. If a player intentionally turns his body to create contact with his back, a penalty may not be called.

Checking from behind is unacceptable at any level of hockey—it is dangerous and is absolutely forbidden in organized youth hockey. Don't check from behind. Let your opponent skate away. It's the right and only way to play.

<u>Rule 49.</u> Clipping

(a) *A player may not deliver a check in a "clipping" manner, nor lower his own body to deliver a check on or below an opponent's knees.*

(b) *An illegal "low hit" is any check with an intent to contact the opposing player in the area of his knees.*

A player who commits these fouls will be given a two-minute penalty for "clipping." If an injury occurs, the player will receive a five-minute major and a game misconduct.

Clipping is the act of throwing the body, from any direction, across or below the knees of an opposing player.

Rule 51. Delaying the Game

(a) A two-minute penalty shall be called on any player or goalkeeper who delays the game by deliberately shooting or knocking the puck out of the playing area with his stick, or for throwing or batting it out with his hand.

(c) A two-minute penalty shall be called on any player or goalkeeper who delays the game by deliberately knocking the goal post from its normal position. If the goal post is deliberately displaced by a goalie during a breakaway, a penalty shot shall be awarded. A penalty shot is also awarded if there is not enough time left in the game to serve a two-minute penalty.

(e) A two-minute bench penalty shall be called against any team that, after being warned by the referee, fails to send the correct number of players to the ice to begin play.

BUT HONESTLY, I DIDN'T MEAN TO BAT THE PUCK OUT OF PLAY!

In the early days of hockey, players were expected to remain on the ice for the entire 60 minutes of a game. In those days, it was a common practice for players to shoot the puck into the stands to relieve pressure or to give themselves a few minutes rest. Fans were never happy with the move.

❹ ## Rule 52. Deliberate Injury of Opponents

(a) *A match penalty shall be called on a player who deliberately injures an opponent in any manner. The player shall also be automatically suspended from further action until the Commissioner has ruled on the issue.*

(d) *A game misconduct shall be called on any player who deliberately injures an official, manager, coach, or trainer in any way, and the circumstances shall be reported to the Commissioner for further action.*

The deliberate injury of opponents has always been of great concern to hockey executives. Any sport played with an instrument in the hands, be it a hockey stick or a baseball bat, is bound to have incidents in which an athlete loses control. Players who deliberately injure their opponents have always been dealt with quickly and harshly, though only one player has ever been banned from the NHL for life—Billy Coutu back in 1927, for assaulting a referee in the Stanley Cup Finals.

The deliberate attempt to injure has no place in hockey. Every player is responsible to himself and his teammates to play clean hockey within the rules.

Rule 54. Face-offs

(a) *The puck shall be faced-off by the referee or the linesman dropping the puck on the ice between the sticks of the players facing-off. Players facing-off will stand squarely facing their opponent's end of the rink, approximately one stick length apart with the blades of their sticks on the ice.*

Two wingers (circled) illegally enter the face-off circle before the drop of the puck.

When the face-off takes place in any of the end face-off circles, the players taking part will stand squarely facing their opponent's end of the rink and clear of the markings on the ice. The sticks of both players facing-off shall have their blades on the ice, within the designated white area of the face-off circle. The visiting player shall place his stick on the ice first.

No other player shall be allowed to enter the face-off circle or come within 15 feet of the players facing-off.

(b) If, after a warning by the referee or linesman, either of the players fails to promptly take his proper position for the face-off, the official shall be entitled to drop the puck even if the player is not yet ready.

(c) During a face-off anywhere on the ice, no player taking the face-off shall make any physical contact with his opponent's body with either *his own body or his stick except in the course of playing the puck after the face-off has been completed.*

(d) *If a player facing-off fails to take his proper position immediately when directed by the official, the official may order him replaced for that face-off by any teammate that is then on the ice.*

(e) *A second violation of any of the previous sections of this rule shall result in a two-minute penalty to the player who commits the second violation.*

At the beginning of each period and after every stoppage in play, a face-off is used to resume play. In the early days of hockey, play would begin with the referee placing the puck on the ice between the sticks of the two centermen, then shouting, "Play!" Often, the two centers would swing their sticks wildly and bang the referee on his legs. Eventually, referees began dropping the puck in order to give themselves a little more time to clear away. Fred Waghorn, a member of the Hockey Hall of Fame, is credited with being the first referee to drop the puck instead of placing it on the ice. Players used to crowd tightly around the two face-off combatants until the 1934–35 season, when rules were passed to keep other teammates at least 10 feet away from the center. Prior to the 1942–43 season, the two players taking the face-off faced the sides of the rink when they lined up.

Rule 55. **Falling on Puck**

(a) *A two-minute penalty shall be called on any player other than the goalkeeper who deliberately falls on the puck or gathers the puck into his body.*

Note: Any player who drops to his knees to block a shot should not be penalized if the puck is shot under him or becomes lodged in his clothing or equipment.

(b) *A two-minute penalty shall be called on a goalkeeper who deliberately falls on the puck, or gathers the puck into his body while in his crease with no players from the other team around him.*

PUCK? WHAT PUCK?

(c) *No defending player except the goalkeeper will be allowed to fall on the puck, hold the puck, or gather the puck into the body or hands when the puck is within the goal crease.*

For breaking this rule, play shall immediately be stopped and a penalty shot shall be ordered against the offending team.

At no time in hockey history has a player been allowed to fall on the puck without being penalized. In the early days of hockey, not even goalies were allowed to fall on the puck.

Rule 57. Goals and Assists

(a) *A goal shall be scored when the puck is put between the goal posts by the stick of an attacking player held below the level of the crossbar on the net. The puck must entirely cross the red line drawn between the goal posts, and the goal frame must be in its proper position.*

(b) *A goal shall be scored if the puck is put into the goal in any way by a player of the defending side. The player of the attacking side who* last played the puck shall be credited with the goal, but no assist shall be awarded.

(c) A goal cannot be scored by an attacking player who deliberately bats the puck with any part of his body. A goal cannot be scored when a player bats the puck and it deflects off any other player or goalkeeper into the net.

(d) If an attacking player has the puck deflect into the net off his skate or body in any way, the goal shall be allowed. The player who deflected the puck shall be credited with the goal.

The goal shall not be allowed if the puck has been intentionally kicked into the net and a distinct kicking motion is evident.

(e) If a goal is scored as a result of being deflected directly into the net off of a referee or a linesman, the goal shall not be allowed.

(h) A goal shall be credited in the scoring records to any player who scores. Each goal shall count for one point in the player's record.

(i) When a player scores a goal, an assist shall be credited to the player or players taking part in the play immediately preceding the goal. No more than two assists can be awarded on one goal. Each assist counts for one point in the player's record.

(j) Only one point can be credited to any player on any one goal.

Pavel Bure won the 1999–2000 goal-scoring race with 58 goals.

4

The rules concerning how a goal can be scored have changed very little over the years. Goals have never been allowed if they are knocked in with a high stick, but what constitutes a high stick has been adjusted on several occasions. For a long time, a high stick meant any stick that was raised above the level of a player's shoulder. Currently, the height of the top of the crossbar on the net is used to indicate a high stick.

Determining who has scored a goal is not always easy. In 1947–48, the NHL asked any player who scored a goal to raise his stick (much in the way players still celebrate a goal today). When a goal is scored, one or two assists can also be awarded to those teammates of the goal scorer who took part in the play immediately preceding the goal. Today, it is the official scorer's duty to determine who should be credited with goals and assists. Assists were first officially recorded as a statistic by the Pacific Coast Hockey Association in 1914 but did not become official in the NHL until the 1918–19 season. From 1930–31 to 1935–36, three assists could be awarded on a goal. The current system of allowing only two assists was introduced in 1936–37. In the NHL, a player does not have to make a direct pass to another player in order to record an assist. He can still get an assist if his pass bounces off a defending player, or if his shot is stopped by the goalie and a teammate bangs in the rebound. No player can be credited with a goal and an assist on the same play, even if the goal scorer first passed the puck to another player who then passed it back to him. No player can be credited with two assists on the same goal.

Every goal and every assist count as one point in a player's scoring record. When a player is said to have scored 60 points, this means that his total number of goals and assists equals 60. At the end of each season, the NHL awards the Art Ross Trophy to the player with the most points and the Maurice "Rocket" Richard Trophy to the leading goal scorer. The Art Ross Trophy is one of the oldest awards in hockey. Jaromir Jagr of the Pittsburgh Penguins has won it four times, including 1998–99 and 1999–2000. The Maurice "Rocket" Richard Trophy was first awarded in 1998–99. Teemu Selanne of the Mighty Ducks of Anaheim won it that year. Pavel Bure of the Florida Panthers won it in 1999–2000. Wayne Gretzky holds the NHL records for goals, assists, and points in a single season and in a career. Gretzky scored 92 goals in 1980-81, 163 assists in 1985-86, and 215 points in 1985-86. His career totals of 894 goals, 1,963 assists, and 2,857 points lead all NHL scorers. Gordie Howe, the second-highest scorer in NHL history, trails Gretzky's amazing career total by 1,050 points.

Rule 59. Handling Puck with Hands

(a) *If a player, except a goalkeeper, closes his hand on the puck, the play shall be stopped and a two-minute penalty called. A goalkeeper who holds the puck with his hands for longer than three seconds when no opposing player is nearby shall receive a two-minute penalty.*

(b) *A goalkeeper cannot throw the puck forward toward the opponent's net, nor deliberately pile up snow or obstacles at or near his net that in the opinion of the referee would tend to prevent the scoring of a goal.*

(d) *A two-minute penalty shall be called on a player, except the goalkeeper, who picks up the puck off the ice with his hands while play is in progress.*

If a player, except a goalkeeper, picks up the puck with his hand in the goal crease, a penalty shot shall be awarded to the non-offending team.

(e) *A player shall be permitted to stop or "bat" a puck in the air with his open hand or push it along the ice with his hand. However, play will be stopped if the referee feels a player has used his hand to deliberately direct the puck to a teammate in any zone but the defensive zone.*

Until the 1927–28 season, the NHL had no rule to penalize a player for closing his hand on the puck. Many old-timers followed the example of Fred "Cyclone" Taylor of the Vancouver Millionaires who would sometimes pick up the puck and throw it into the crowd to relieve pressure or give his team a rest. The current version of the rule was introduced in 1951–52. Until then, players could not close their hand on the puck for more than three seconds, but they could catch

To stop play, many old-time players like Fred "Cyclone" Taylor would throw the puck into the stands.

it in the air and hand it to the referee to stop the play.

Though it has rarely been called as a penalty, NHL goalies are not allowed to throw the puck forward. The rule against piling up snow in front of the net passed after Chris Osgood of the Detroit Red Wings did just that to help stop a penalty shot on April 1, 1995.

Rule 65. Icing the Puck

(a) *For the purposes of this rule, the center red line will divide the ice into halves. Except when a team is shorthanded due to a penalty, if any player shoots, bats, or deflects the puck from his half of the ice*

beyond the goal line of the opposing team, play shall be stopped as soon as a member of the opposing team touches the puck. A face-off will be held in the defensive end of the offending team. It is not considered to be icing if a goal is scored on the play.

I MEANT ICE THE PUCK.

(b) If a player on the offensive team who is not offside should reach the puck before an opposing player, icing is not called and the play continues.

(d) If the puck goes beyond the goal line in the opposite end of the ice directly from a face-off, this shall not be considered icing.

(e) If the linesman believes a player from the opposing team is able to catch up to the puck before it passes his goal line, icing shall not be called.

(f) If the puck touches any part of a player of the opposing team, or passes through the goal crease before it crosses that team's goal line, the play shall not be considered icing. If the puck touches any part of the opposing team's goalkeeper, it is not icing.

(g) If the puck passes through the crease after the other team has pulled its goalie for an extra attacker, then icing shall be called on the play.

The icing rule was passed by the NHL Board of Governors on September 24, 1937. Prior to that date, some teams that gained an early lead would shoot the puck all the way down to the other end of the ice at every opportunity in order to protect their advantage. Once, in a game played on November 8, 1931, the New York Americans iced the puck more than 50 times in order to protect a 3–2 lead. The Boston Bruins were so angry that the next time they played the Americans (December 3, 1931), they iced the puck 87 times! The game ended in a 0–0 tie.

Rule 70. **Kicking the Puck**

(a) *Kicking the puck shall be permitted in all zones, but a goal cannot be scored by an attacking player who uses a deliberate kicking motion to propel the puck into the net. A goal cannot be scored by an attacking player who kicks a puck that deflects into the net off any player, goalkeeper, or official.*

(b) *A puck that deflects into the net off of an attacking player who does not use a distinct kicking motion is a goal.*

(c) *A goal cannot be scored by an attacking player who kicks any piece of equipment (stick, glove, helmet, etc.) at the puck, causing the puck to cross the goal line.*

Kicking the puck directly into the net has never been allowed in the game of hockey. In fact, in the very early years of hockey, using skates to move the puck at all was against the rules. By the time the NHL was formed in 1917, kicking the puck was allowed in the neutral zone. In 1927, the NHL allowed players to kick the puck away from the boards. In 1930–31, kicking the puck was allowed anywhere on the ice.

NICE KICK. WRONG SPORT!

Rule 74. Offsides

(a) *The position of the player's skates and not that of his stick shall be the determining factor in all instances in deciding an offside. A player is offside when both skates are completely over the outer edge of the determining center line or blue line involved in the play.*

(b) *If in the opinion of the linesman an intentional offside play has been made, the face-off shall take place at the other end of the ice in the defending zone of the team that was offside.*

Rule 75. Passes

(a) *The puck may be passed by any player to a player on the same team within any one of the three zones into which the ice is divided. If the puck is passed forward by a player in one zone to a player on the same team in another zone, the pass is considered offside. However, players on the defending team are allowed to pass the puck to a player on the same team in the neutral zone, provided the pass is completed on the defending team's side of the center ice red line.*

Rule 77. Preceding Puck into Attacking Zone

(a) *Players of the attacking team must not be inside the attacking zone before the puck is brought in.*

(b) *For violation of this rule, the play is stopped and the puck is faced-off outside the blue line in the neutral zone at the face-off spot nearest to where the offside occurred.*

(c)   *If the attacking team shoots the puck in offside but does not have control of the puck, the defending team has the chance to carry the puck back out. A delayed offside is then in effect. The linesman raises his arm but does not blow his whistle. If the defending team carries the puck out of its zone, play continues. If the attacking team touches the puck before it is brought out across the blue line, offside is called and the play is whistled to a stop.*

(d)   *If a player carries or passes the puck back into his own defending zone while a player from the other team is still there, the offside shall be ignored and play permitted to continue.*

In the early days of hockey, there were no lines on the ice, and players were not allowed to pass the puck to any teammate who was in front of them. Player who were ahead of the puck were considered offside and could not touch the puck until it was shot or carried past them. After blue lines were added to the ice—in the PCHA in 1913–14, and in the NHL in 1917–18—forward passing was allowed in the defensive zone and later in the neutral zone. It wasn't until the 1929–30 season, however, that forward passing was allowed everywhere on the ice. As forward passing rules were changed, rules about offside also had to be changed. To make sure

that players didn't just hang around the other team's net all the time and wait for teammates to get the puck to them, rules were passed that said no player could cross the other team's blue line ahead of the puck. At this time, no pass could be made from one zone to another. When the center ice red line was introduced in 1943–44, rules were changed to allow the defending team to pass the puck from its own zone into the neutral zone—as long as the pass was completed before the puck crossed center ice. This made passing even more important. Many people consider the 1943–44 season to be the beginning of "the modern age of hockey."

The linesman has the job of deciding if a play is offside, while he and the puck and the players are moving at high speeds. If one skate of a player touches the blue line or red line, he is onside. If a player carries the puck on his stick ahead of his skates, he is onside when he crosses the blue line because the puck crossed first. If the puck is in the attacking zone and is passed back to the blue line, it has to completely cross the blue line to be considered out of the zone. If even a tiny piece of the puck is still touching the blue-painted ice, the puck is still considered to be inside the attacking zone.

Rule 78. Protection of Goalkeeper

(a) *If an attacking player creates contact with a goalkeeper, accidentally or on purpose, while the goalkeeper is in his goal crease and a goal is scored, the goal will be disallowed.*

(b) *If an attacking player creates contact with a goalkeeper (unless it is minor) while the goalkeeper is outside his goal crease and a goal is scored, the goal will be disallowed.*

(c) *In all cases in which an attacking player purposely makes contact with a goalkeeper, whether the goalkeeper is in his crease or not, and whether or not a goal is scored, the offensive player will receive a penalty of either two minutes or five minutes as determined by the referee.*

   If an attacking player has been pushed or shoved so as to come into contact with the goalkeeper, no penalty shall be called provided that the attacking player has made a reasonable effort to avoid such contact.

   A goalkeeper is not considered "fair game" just because he is outside his crease. The appropriate penalty should be called in every case where an attacking player makes unnecessary contact with a goalkeeper.

(d) *Even if a goalkeeper causes contact with an attacking player in order to establish his position in the crease and a goal is scored while the two are in contact, the goal shall be disallowed.*

(e) *If an attacking player does not immediately leave the crease after contact with a goalkeeper who is trying to establish his position and a goal is scored, the goal shall be disallowed. Whether a goal is scored or not, the player shall receive a two-minute penalty for goalkeeper interference.*

THIS PROTECTING OF THE GOALIE HAS GONE A LITTLE TOO FAR.

(f) *When a goalkeeper has played the puck outside of his crease and is then prevented from returning to his crease by the deliberate actions of an attacking player, such a player may be penalized. Similarly, a goaltender may be penalized if he interferes with an attacking player.*

(g) *If an attacking player sets himself up inside the goal crease in such a way as to block a goalkeeper's vision of the play and a goal is scored, the goal will be disallowed.*

(h) *If an attacking player sets himself up inside the goal crease in such a way as to block the goalkeeper's ability to move and defend his goal, and a goal is scored, the goal shall be disallowed.*

(i) *In a rebound situation, or when a goalkeeper and an attacking player are both trying to play a loose puck at the same time, any minor contact inside the crease or out will be allowed, and any goal scored under these circumstances will be allowed.*

(j) *In the event that a goalkeeper has been pushed into the net together with the puck after making a stop, the goal will be disallowed. If appropriate, a penalty will be called.*

(k) *A goalkeeper who deliberately causes contact with an attacking player, other than to establish his position in the crease, is subject to a penalty.*

(l) *An attacking player who, in the judgment of the referee, causes contact with the goalkeeper whether inside the crease or out, will receive a penalty.*

Since goal creases were added to the ice in 1934–35, the size has changed from time to time in order to provide better protection for the goalies. In 1991–92, even stronger rules to protect goaltenders were introduced to the NHL. By the late 1990s, the rules had become so strict that if any part of an attacking player was in the crease when a goal was scored, whether it interfered with the play or not, the goal would not count. Video goal judges would often be used to review goals and determine if a player was in the crease. Beginning in 1999–2000, the rules were changed so that any goal scored would count unless a player on the attacking team interfered with the goalie on purpose. Only the referee on the ice was allowed to make the call.

Rule 82. Puck Striking Official

(a)   Play shall not be stopped if the puck touches an official anywhere on the rink. However, play will be stopped if the puck bouncing off a referee or linesman causes a player to be offside (see Rule 74).

> <u>Note:</u> *If a goal is scored as a result of being deflected off an official directly into the net, the goal shall not be allowed.*

Prior to the 1940–41 season, play stopped immediately whenever the puck hit a referee or linesman, and a face-off was held where play was stopped. Then, a rule was passed that allowed play to continue if the puck hit an official in the neutral zone. In 1945, the rule was expanded to allow play to continue if the puck hit an official anywhere on the ice. Despite all the changes, a goal has never been allowed to count if the puck enters the net after deflecting off a referee or linesman.

O.K.! WHO'S THE WISE GUY?

<u>Rule 88.</u> Throwing Stick

(a) When any member of the defending team, including players, coaches, managers, and trainers, deliberately throws or shoots any part of a stick or any other object at the puck or the puck carrier in his team's defending zone, the referee shall allow the play to be completed. If no goal is scored, a penalty shot will be awarded to the player who has been fouled. If the defending team has pulled its goalie and the attacking player is prevented from having a clear shot at the "open net," a goal shall be awarded to the attacking team.

(b) A two-minute penalty will be called against any player who throws or shoots any part of a stick or any object in the direction of the puck, unless the result of the play should be a penalty shot or an awarded goal.

(c) A misconduct or a game misconduct penalty (determined by the referee) will be called against any player who throws any part of his stick off the ice into the stands or a bench.

In the early days of hockey, a player who threw his stick at the puck or the puck carrier would receive a game misconduct. By the time the NHL was formed in 1917–18, the rule had been changed to say that any time a player threw his stick, the other team would be awarded a goal. This rule was changed during the 1930s, when the penalty shot was first introduced.

Today, throwing a stick will only result in an automatic goal if the net is empty.

Rule 89. Tied Game

(a) *During regular-season NHL games, if the score is tied at the end of three regular 20-minute periods, each team shall be awarded one point in the standings.*

The teams will then play an additional overtime period of not more than five minutes with the team scoring first declared the winner and being awarded an additional point. The team that gets one point for losing will have this listed as a "regulation tie" in the standings. During overtime, each team will have only four skaters and one goalkeeper on the ice.

Note 1: If a team is penalized in overtime, teams will play four skaters against three.

Note 2: In overtime, if a team gets two penalties and has to play two men short, instead of playing four skaters against two, the penalized team with three skaters will keep three skaters on the ice while the team with four skaters will be allowed to add a fifth man.

Note 5: A team is allowed to pull its goalie during overtime in favor of an additional skater, but if that team gives up a goal and loses the game, it will not receive the one point it is otherwise entitled to for the tie.

Hockey games are made up of three 20-minute periods. Youth hockey games are often shorter, with periods of 12 or 15 minutes. Between periods the ice is resurfaced, and the teams change ends. In NHL

In 1942, NHL president Frank Calder changed the rules, banning overtime games.

regular-season games, when the score is tied after the third period, a five-minute overtime period is played. The ice isn't resurfaced and the teams don't change ends between the third period and the start of overtime. If a team scores a goal in the overtime period, the game is over.

Regular-season overtime was originally a feature of the NHL when the League was formed in 1917–18. Up until the 1920–21 season, overtime was played until a team won the game—no matter how long it took. In 1921–22, the League decided that if a game was still tied after 20 minutes of overtime, it would remain a tie.

In 1928–29, the NHL eliminated sudden-death overtime. If a game was tied after three periods, teams would then play an overtime period that would last 10 minutes no matter how many goals were scored. The record for most goals scored in a overtime period was four. Ken Doraty of the Toronto Maple Leafs, who only scored 15 goals in his whole career, once scored a hat trick (three goals) in one overtime period! On November 21, 1942, NHL president Frank Calder announced that the League would no longer play overtime games in the regular season. In those days, teams all traveled by train, and it was common practice to delay the trains if a hockey game went into overtime. But with World War II in progress, it was more important for the trains to run on time. As a result, the NHL stopped playing overtime games. It wasn't until 1983 that the NHL started using overtime again. This time, the League decided that teams would play a five-minute sudden-death period if a game was tied after 60 minutes. The first team to score won the game. They would get two points, and the loser would get zero. If neither team scored, the game would end in a tie, and both teams would get one point.

Beginning with the 1999-2000 season, the team that scored in overtime was credited with a win. The team that lost in overtime was credited with a loss but also received a bonus point in the standings for the tie at the end of regulation time. Also new for 1999–2000 was the use of four skaters for each team instead of five in the overtime frame. The idea was to make the play more exciting with greater scoring chances. The four-on-four approach seems to have worked. In 1998–99, when overtime was still played five-on-five, 27 percent of overtime games ended with a goal scored; in 1999–2000, when overtime was four on four, approximately 43 percent of overtime games ended with a goal scored.

The bonus point for overtime wins resulted in a new way of listing each team's results in the standings tables published in the newspapers or on hockey websites each day. Here is a sample line from the new standings:

Team	GP	W	L	T	RT	Pts.
New Jersey	82	45	29	8	5	103

GP = Games Played; **W** = Wins; **L** = Losses; **T** = Ties;
RT = Regulation Ties; **Pts.** = Total Points Earned

In the example above, the regulation ties are games that New Jersey tied at the end of regulation time and then lost in overtime. Losses in overtime are recorded as losses in the standings table as well. Each win is worth 2 points (45 wins x 2 points per win = 90 points); each tie is

Brett Hull celebrates his 1998–99 Stanley Cup-winning overtime goal with his teammates.

worth 1 point (8 ties x 1 point per tie = 8 points); each regulation tie is worth 1 point (5 regulation ties x 1 point = 5 points). Total points are calculated by adding the points for wins, ties, and regulation ties (90 + 8 + 5 = 103). Games played are calculated by adding wins, losses, and ties. Regulation ties are not counted when adding up games played because they are included in the loss column.

Overtime in the Stanley Cup Playoffs is very different from overtime in the regular season. In the playoffs, additional 20-minute overtime periods are played until a goal is scored, even if many overtime periods are required. Teams play with five skaters a side in playoff overtime—unless there are penalties.

The longest playoff game ever recorded took place on March 24, 1936. The Detroit Red Wings and Montreal Maroons needed 116 minutes and 30 seconds of extra time before Mud Bruneteau finally scored for Detroit. That's almost six full overtime periods! More recently, on May 4, 2000, the Philadelphia Flyers and Pittsburgh Penguins played 92 minutes and 1 second of overtime before Keith Primeau of the Flyers scored. And the New Jersey Devils needed two overtime periods to become Stanley Cup Champions in 2000. Jason

Arnott scored at 8:20 of the second overtime period to give the Devils a 2–1 victory over the Dallas Stars in Game Six of the Stanley Cup Finals.

Rule 90. **Time of Match**

(a)   The time allowed for a game shall be three 20-minute periods of actual playing time with a rest intermission between periods.

Play shall be resumed promptly following each intermission once 15 minutes are up. Timing of the intermission begins as soon as the players and officials leave the ice at the end of a period.

(b)   The team that scores the most goals during the three 20-minute periods is the winner and receives two points in the standings.

(c)   In the intermission between periods, the ice shall be flooded unless both teams agree that it should not be.

When the first rules of hockey were written down back in the 1870s, the game was 60 minutes long just like today, but instead of three 20-minute periods it had two 30-minute halves. Players got a 10-minute break between halves. Before the 1910–11 season, the National Hockey Association (the forerunner of the NHL) changed the rules to make the game into three periods since players were expected to be on the ice for all 60 minutes of the game. The league thought that shorter periods with an extra time to rest would keep the players from getting too tired and therefore keep the game moving faster. Only minor changes have been made to this rule over the years. The most significant came in 1966–67, when the length of the intermission between periods was extended from 10 minutes to 15.

One of the most important—but often overlooked—rule changes in hockey concerned resurfacing the ice. Prior to the 1940–41 season, the ice was only flooded at the beginning of each game. Between periods, attendants would scrape the excess snow off the ice, but no attempts were made to completely clean and resurface the ice. Beginning in 1940, however, the ice was flooded between each period. At first, the job required a crew of 8 to 10 people with large metal scrapers to remove the snow and another group to wheel around large barrels that spread a coat of hot water over the ice so the surface would refreeze more smoothly. The first man to invent a motorized machine for cleaning ice was named Frank Zamboni. The first NHL rink to use the new machine—called a Zamboni—was the Montreal Forum on March 10, 1955. By the early 1960s, every NHL rink had a Zamboni. Soon the Zamboni was as much a part of the atmosphere of the hockey arena as the organist, score clock, and vendors selling snacks.

In 1994–95, the NHL passed a rule that required teams to use two ice resurfacing machines between periods to allow more time for on-ice promotions and displays.

Rule 92. Time-Outs

Each team shall be permitted to take one 30-second time-out during any game, regular-season or playoff. This time-out must be taken during a normal stoppage of play.

Note 1: All players including goalkeepers on the ice at the time of the time-out will be allowed to go to their respective benches. Only one team is allowed a time-out per stoppage in play.

Since there are so many times in an NHL game when the play is stopped, many fans were surprised when the League introduced a time-out rule in 1983. It was designed to be used in close games, when a coach was planning to pull his goaltender or set up a strategic face-off play. Since then, it has become an important piece of game strategy. A properly called time-out allows a coach to keep his number-one line on the ice for a double shift in the final minutes of a game, or it can allow penalty killers to get an important rest. It also can allow both teams to set up their defenses for an all-important face-off in the dying seconds. Sometimes a coach will simply call a time-out if he feels the momentum of the game is switching toward the other team.

<u>Rule 93.</u> Video Goal Judge

The following questions and situations can be reviewed by the video goal judge:

(a) *Did the puck cross the goal line?*

(b) *Was the puck in the net before the goal frame was knocked off?*

(c) *Was the puck in the net before time ran out in the period?*

(d) *Was the puck directed into the net by a hand or foot? With the use of the foot or skate, was a distinct kicking motion used?*

(e) *Did the puck deflect into the net off of an official?*

(f) *Was the puck struck with a high stick (above the height of the crossbar) before it went into the net?*

(g) *What was the correct time on the official game clock (provided the game time was visible on the video goal judge's monitor)?*

4 Video replays in the NHL were introduced prior to the 1991–92 season and generally were used only to determine whether or not a goal should count. But, in 1994–95, the video goal judge was allowed to help determine the official time of the game as well. The use of video replays became controversial when it was used to call back goals if any part of a player or his equipment was in the goal crease when a goal was scored. When this rule was modified before the 1999–2000 season to state that a player could be in the crease as long as he didn't interfere with the goalie, the decision was left completely up to the referee on the ice.

You're at a local hockey game, reading your copy of *Hockey Rules!* in the stands. Suddenly, the referee gets injured and has to leave the ice. The players and coaches notice the rulebook in your hands, and come to you for help. You are now the referee. You make the calls!

YOU MAKE THE CALLS!

Rule 42

Q: *A goalkeeper requires a quick adjustment to the straps on his leg pads. Must he remain at his net or can he go to the bench without being replaced?*

A: *A goalkeeper may not got to the bench without being replaced, even if the delay is a short one. The goalie must be replaced by his backup and cannot return until the next stoppage in play. (Sometimes, though, if he gets permission from the referee, a goalkeeper can make quick fixes on the ice or go to the bench without being replaced—provided the delay is very short.)*

Rule 43

Q: *A player from team A deliberately shoots the puck into the team B bench in an attempt to hit an opponent. What penalty would be called?*

A: *A match penalty for attempt to injure should be called. However, if the player shot the puck into the bench to start a fight and not actually to hurt someone, he would receive a misconduct penalty.*

Rule 45

Q: *Can a player who has broken his stick receive a replacement from a teammate in the penalty box?*

A: *No. The player who receives the new stick would receive a two-minute penalty.*

Q: *A goalkeeper breaks his stick and a teammate on the bench throws a new one onto the ice. A player picks it up and gives it to the goalie. What penalties would be called?*

A: *The player who threw the stick onto the ice receives a two-minute bench penalty. There is no penalty given to the goalie or the player who picked up the stick.*

Q: *A player taking a new stick to his goalie slides it to him along the ice and into the crease. The goalie does not have time to pick it up before an opposing player fires a shot. The stick prevents the shot from going into the net. Should a penalty shot be awarded?*

A: *Because the stick was not thrown at the puck or the puck carrier, no penalty shot would be awarded. The goalie would not receive a penalty because he did not place the stick in front of the net.*

Rule 48

Q: *A player on team A, who is unable to defend himself, is cross-checked from behind into the boards by a player on team B. What penalty should be called?*

A: *The player on team B should be given a five-minute major penalty and a game misconduct (there is no minor penalty for hitting from behind). However, if the hit is not considered serious, the referee can give the player a two-minute penalty for cross-checking instead of calling a penalty for hitting from behind.*

Q: *A player from team A is carrying the puck along the boards and sees a player from team B who is about to check him. The team A player turns around to create contact with his back. Should the referee call a penalty for checking from behind?*

A: *No. The player from team A was aware that a hit was coming and turned his back intentionally. However, if the hit from behind broke another rule (slashing or cross-checking, for example), the appropriate penalty should be called, even though the team A player put himself in a vulnerable position.*

Rule 49

Q: *A player from team A dives at a player from team B, striking him in the shins and knocking him down. Is this a penalty?*

A: *Yes. The player from team A should get two minutes for clipping.*

Rule 51

Q: *A goalkeeper makes a save and the puck bounces into the air. In trying to clear the puck, the goalie bats it into the stands. Should a delay of game penalty be called?*

A: *No. This is not considered to be an illegal act, since the goalkeeper didn't intentionally try to delay the game.*

Q: *Team A is applying pressure to team B. A team B defender decides to relieve the pressure and deliberately shoots the puck out of the playing area with his stick. What penalty should be called?*

A: *A two-minute penalty for delay of game.*

Q: The net is deliberately knocked off its moorings by the goalie just as an attacking player is shooting the puck. What happens?

A: *If the attacking player shoots the puck and it crosses the goal line between the normal position of the posts, the referee will award a goal. If no shot is actually made, the referee calls a two-minute penalty. If there is not enough time left in the game for the penalty to be served, a penalty shot will be awarded.*

Rule 52

Q: *What penalty should be called against any player who deliberately attempts to injure another player?*

A: *A match penalty. The NHL Commissioner would then decide on an appropriate suspension.*

Q: *What penalty should be called against any player who deliberately attempts to injure a referee or a coach?*

A: *A game misconduct. The NHL Commissioner would then decide on an appropriate suspension.*

Rule 54

Q: *Which team's player must place his stick down first on all face-offs?*

A: *The visiting team's player.*

You Make the Calls!

Q: *While the puck is in the crease, a player outside of the crease covers it with his hand. Should a penalty shot be called?*

A: *Yes. It is the position of the puck that counts—not the position of the player.*

Q: *A defending player is in the crease, but the puck is outside of it. The player pulls the puck into the crease and covers it. What should be called?*

A: *Because the puck was originally outside the crease, a two-minute penalty should be called.*

Q: *A defending player who is outside the crease pulls the puck out of the crease and falls on it. What is the proper call?*

A: *A penalty shot should be awarded because the puck was in the crease when the infraction occured.*

Q: *A team has pulled its goaltender and a defenseman has taken a position inside the goal crease. While the player is standing in the crease, the puck is shot toward the goal and the defenseman covers it. What is the proper call?*

A: *If the player intentionally covered the puck, a penalty shot should be called.*

Rule 57

Q: *An attacking player deliberately kicks the puck, which deflects off a defending player into the net. Does the goal count?*

A: *No. A goal cannot be scored when a player deliberately bats the puck or uses a distinct kicking motion to put it in the net, even if the puck bounces in off of someone else.*

Q: *An attacking player deliberately kicks the puck using a distinct kicking motion. The puck then makes contact with his own or a teammate's stick and goes into the net. Does the goal count?*

A: *Yes. If an attacking player has the puck deflect into the net off his body in any way, the goal shall be allowed. The player who deflected the puck will be credited with the goal.*

Rule 59

Q: *A player in the defending zone bats the puck to a teammate in the neutral zone. Should play be stopped?*

A: *Yes. The play is stopped as soon as the teammate takes possession of the puck in the neutral zone. The face-off takes place at the spot where the puck was batted.*

Q: *A player on the attacking team bats the puck into the corner of the attacking zone. A teammate skates into the corner and picks it up. What is the proper call?*

A: *If the referee believes the puck was batted deliberately, he should blow the whistle and stop the play. If the puck was not batted deliberately, the play should be permitted to continue.*

Q: *A player closes his hand on the puck, takes two strides to avoid a check, then drops the puck and plays it. Is this legal?*

A: *No. A two-minute penalty for handling the puck should be called. A player may not gain an advantage over an opponent by closing his hand on the puck.*

Rule 65

Q: *A player on team A attempts to ice the puck with one second left in a teammate's penalty. By the time a team B player touches the puck, the penalty has expired. Should icing be called?*

A: *No. The determining time is when the puck is shot, not when it is touched.*

Rule 70

Q: *The puck is kicked with a distinct kicking motion and deflects off an official and into the net. Goal or no goal?*

A: *No goal. A goal cannot be scored by an attacking player who kicks a puck that deflects into the net off any player, goalkeeper, or official.*

Q: *An attacking player has the puck on the blade of his stick but is unable to shoot in a normal manner. He deliberately kicks the blade of his stick, which knocks the puck into the opponent's net. Goal or no goal?*

A: *No goal. A goal cannot be scored by an attacking player who kicks any piece of equipment (stick, glove, helmet, etc.) at the puck.*

Q: *An attacking player shoots the puck at his opponent's net. A teammate in front of the net sees the puck coming and deliberately turns his skate, which causes the puck to deflect off it and into the net. Goal or no goal?*

A: *Goal. Even though the move was deliberate, there was no distinct kicking motion.*

Rule 74

Q: *An attacking player is struggling to stay onside. He has one foot in the attacking zone and one foot on the blue line as a teammate brings the puck in. Is he offside?*

A: *No. Both skates must be over the line for a player to be offside.*

Q: *An attacking player is struggling to stay onside. He has one foot in the attacking zone and one foot in the air above the blue line as a teammate brings the puck in. Is he offside?*

A: *Yes. A player must have his skate actually in contact with the blue line in order to be considered onside.*

Q: *A player in possession of the puck crosses the blue line into the attacking zone while skating backward. Since his skates actually precede the puck across the blue line, is he offside?*

A: *This is a bit of a trick question, because the rule says it is the position of a player's skates that determines if he is offside. However, if the player actually has possession and control of the puck while he is skating backward, he is not considered offside.*

Q: *A player on the attacking team is pushed over the blue line by a player on the defending team, causing him to go offside. Is the play offside?*

A: *Yes. Offside should still be called, but the defending player should be given a two-minute penalty for interference.*

Rule 75

Q: *A player in the defensive zone passes the puck to a teammate in the neutral zone. The teammate is on the other side of the center ice red line. Is this a legal pass?*

A: *No. This pass would be considered offside. A player in the defending zone is allowed to pass the puck into the neutral zone, but only if his teammate is on their side of the center ice red line.*

Rule 77

Q: *A player from team A carries the puck back into his own defending zone while a player from team B is still there. Is the team B player offside?*

A: *No. Even though players of the attacking team must not be inside the attacking zone before the puck is brought in, if a player carries or passes the puck back into his own defending zone (the other team's attacking zone) while a player from the other team is still there, the offside shall be ignored.*

Rule 78

Q: *A player on team A knocks the stick out of the hands of team B's goalkeeper. Should a penalty be called?*

A: *Yes. A player who knocks the stick out of a goalie's hands should be given a penalty for interference or slashing.*

Q: *An attacking player is standing in the crease when a goal is scored. The player has not affected the goalkeeper's ability to defend his net. Does the goal count?*

A: *Yes. For a goal to be called back, an attacking player has to make contact with the goalie, or be standing deliberately in his way inside the crease.*

Q: *An attacking player accidentally bumps into the goalkeeper in the crease at the same time that a goal is scored. Does the goal count?*

A: *No. A goal cannot be scored if a player has contacted the goalie either accidentally or on purpose. The referee should call a two-minute penalty.*

Q: *A player accidentally bumps into the goalkeeper outside the crease at the same time that a goal is scored. Does the goal count?*

A: *Yes. If the goalie is outside of the crease, contact must be deliberate for the goal to be disallowed.*

Q: *After making a reasonable effort to get out of the way after being pushed by a defenseman, an attacking player makes contact with the goalkeeper and a goal is scored. Does the goal count?*

A: *Yes. If an attacking player has been pushed or shoved into the goalkeeper, no penalty shall be called provided that the attacking player has made a reasonable effort to avoid contact.*

Rule 82

Q: *A puck hits an official and goes directly into the net. Should the goal be allowed?*

A: *No. If a goal is scored as a result of being deflected into the net off an official, the goal shall not be allowed.*

Rule 88

Q: *What is the call if a player in his own defensive zone throws his stick or any object at the attacking puck carrier?*

A: *If the attacking player does not score before the play is completed, a penalty shot would be awarded.*

Q: *Team A has pulled their goalkeeper for an extra attacker. A player from team B has a clear shot at the open net, so a player from team A throws his stick, interfering with the shot. What is the call?*

A: *The referee should award a goal.*

Rule 89

Q: *What happens to a team that pulls its goalie in overtime and has a goal scored against it into the open net?*

A: *That team loses the single point normally awarded for a tie.*

Q: *If a team has to serve two penalties at the same time during an overtime period, does it have to play with only two skaters?*

A: *No. If a team gets another penalty while it is shorthanded and playing three skaters against four, the team keeps its three skaters on the ice, but the opposing team is allowed a fifth skater.*

Rule 90

Q: *True or false? Timing for the 15-minute intermission between periods begins as soon as the two teams have reached their dressing rooms.*

A: *False. Timing for the intermission begins as soon as the players and officials have left the ice.*

Rule 92

Q: *Team A has been awarded a penalty shot. After the official has placed the puck at the center ice face-off spot and instructed the shooter and the goalkeeper, team B requests a time-out. Should it be allowed?*

A: *No. A time-out must be taken during a normal stoppage in play.*

5

Q: *Team A requests a time-out during a normal stoppage in play. After the referee blows his whistle to resume play, team B requests a time-out. Should it be allowed?*

A: *No. Only one time-out is allowed per stoppage in play.*

Rule 93

Q: *Can the video goal judge be used to determine if a player interfered with a goalkeeper when a goal was scored?*

A: *No. This situation would not be reviewed by the video goal judge, although it used to be. Now, only the referee is responsible for making this decision.*